Word List

Here is a list of words that might make it easier to read this book. You'll find them in boldface the first time they appear in the story.

Egypt	EE-jipt
archaeology	ar-key-OL-uh-jee
ancient	AYN-shent
tomb	toom
Cairo	KY-roh
pyramids	PIR-uh-mids
pharaohs	FARE-os
tourists	TOOR-ists
pomegranate	POM-uh-gran-it
felucca	fuh-LUKE-uh
hieroglyphics	hy-eruh-GLIF-iks
Arabic	AIR-uh-bik
sphinx	sfingks
linen	LIN-uhn
papyrus	puh-PY-rus
lutes	loots
investigate	in-VES-tuh-gate
sculptors	SKULP-ters
parchment	PARCH-ment
chisel	CHIZ-uhl
disguises	dis-GYZ-ez

Barbie™

The Pyramid Adventure

©1998 Mattel, Inc. Barbie and associated trademarks are owned and used under license from Mattel, Inc. All Rights Reserved. Published by Grolier Enterprises, Inc. Story by Rita Balducci. Photo crew: Willie Lew, Beverly Elam, Cristina LaBianca, James LaBianca, Rory Muir, and Judy Tsuno. Produced by Bumpy Slide Books. Printed in the United States of America.

ISBN: 0-7172-8797-1

Grolier Books

Barbie was very excited. She was going to visit her friend Christie in **Egypt**. Christie was an **archaeology** student studying **ancient** Egypt. She was working with a team of others to uncover a buried **tomb**.

As Barbie looked out the airplane window, she could see the Nile River in the distance.

Just then a voice came over the loudspeaker. "Ladies and gentlemen," said the flight attendant, "we'll soon be landing in **Cairo**. Please put up your tray tables and buckle your seat belts. Thank you for flying with us."

Barbie couldn't believe she was really in Cairo! Egypt was one of the most beautiful lands in the world. Now she could explore it with Christie for the next two weeks. As the plane landed, all Barbie could think about were **pyramids**, mummies, **pharaohs**, and the Nile River. Her only problem was figuring out what to do first.

Barbie gathered her luggage. Then she left the airport and went outside to the street.

"Barbie! Over here!" shouted Christie. "I'm so glad to see you."

"And I'm so glad to be here!" Barbie cried, giving Christie a hug.

The two friends climbed into a taxi. Christie gave the driver directions to Barbie's hotel.

"Look!" Barbie cried. "There goes a man with a camel! It's just like in the movies!"

Christie grinned. "You're going to see a lot of interesting things while you're here, Barbie.

There's never a dull moment in Egypt!"

Slowly the taxi moved through the narrow streets. Barbie was amazed that people, farm animals, bicycles, and buses all shared the same roads.

At last they arrived at the hotel. After Barbie checked in, a bellhop took her bags. Then he led Barbie and Christie to a sunny room with a view of the Nile.

"Ahhhh! Air-conditioning!" Barbie sighed. "It's so hot here. Don't you mind working in the sun all day?"

"Actually, our team works underground," said Christie. "Except for the entrance to the tomb, everything is buried under sand. We've been trying to find all of the tomb's different rooms. But it takes a long time, and we've run into a few dead ends. I can't wait until we finally discover the Treasure Room. It's wonderful to see ancient treasures in a museum. But to find them just as they were left thousands of years ago is almost like going back in time!"

"I hope I get to see the tomb," said Barbie. "Right now, I would love to see what Egypt is like today. Are you ready to give me a tour?"

Christie jumped to her feet. "I know the perfect place to start!" she replied. "There's a wonderful square right in the middle of Cairo."

Barbie grabbed her camera. Then they went out to see the square. It was in the center of a very busy marketplace. Business people rushed past. Barefoot children herded sheep through the streets. People selling jewelry, food, sandals, and rugs were crowded together. Many were shouting out to **tourists** passing by. Barbie had never seen anything like it!

Barbie bought a necklace of tiny seeds and bottles of perfumed oil for her sisters Stacie and Skipper. She found a stuffed camel for her sister Kelly and a keychain with a pyramid on it for her boyfriend, Ken. Feeling hot and thirsty from the bright sun, the two friends stopped to buy a piece of fruit, a juicy red **pomegranate**.

"You had better put this on," Christie said, handing a hat she had in her backpack to Barbie. "You'll need it to block the hot rays of the sun."

Just then a woman gently pushed Barbie out of the way of a passing camel. When Barbie turned to thank her, all she could see were the woman's dark eyes. She was clothed all in black from head to foot. The woman nodded quickly and hurried away through the crowd.

"Wow!" Barbie said as she snapped the last picture on her roll of film. "I had no idea Cairo was so large and busy! I can't wait to see more. But can we go someplace to relax for a few minutes first?"

Christie thought for a minute. "I know where we can go! You'll love this. Follow me!" she said.

Soon Barbie and Christie were seated in a

boat with broad sails. It was called a **felucca**. They sipped limeade and relaxed as the boat drifted its way along the Nile.

"I feel like Cleopatra, the famous Egyptian queen!" giggled Barbie.

"This is the best way to see an Egyptian sunset," Christie said. "And we will be able to get a look at the pyramids from here, too."

"The pyramids!" Barbie cried. "I've always wanted to see them in person."

"Well, you'll get your chance in just a little while," Christie replied. "In the meantime, let's relax and enjoy the view."

Barbie leaned back and watched the sun begin to set. Soon three small triangles appeared in the distance.

"Are those the pyramids?" Barbie asked, pointing ahead.

"Yes!" said Christie. "We know which kings were buried in them with their treasures because it's in the **hieroglyphics**!"

"What are those?" Barbie asked.

"Hieroglyphics are an ancient way of writing that is made up of pictures. If we study them, we can see that the Egyptians had happy lives. They enjoyed their families. They played sports and games. They loved music. And they also had wonderful ceremonies."

Barbie thought about what Christie said. "Maybe we could go to a museum tomorrow," she suggested. "I'd love to see some of the ancient Egyptian treasures that have been found so far."

Christie grinned. "I can do better than that! How about looking for treasures that still remain to be discovered? You could come with me to the tomb site tomorrow. As long as you don't mind being underground, there's always room for one more."

"Then count me in!" Barbie said. What an

exciting trip it was turning out to be!

As the boat headed back to Cairo, Christie said, "Then it's all set. We'll go to the site early in the morning. But first, we'll be sure to stop at a store so you can buy more film!"

Chapter Two

Barbie awoke the next morning to a blazing Egyptian sunrise. It was already very hot, so she dressed in light, cool clothes. Barbie then packed her backpack. She put in her flashlight, camera, sunscreen, and a bottle of water. When Barbie was ready, she hurried down to the hotel lobby. Christie was waiting for her. Barbie just knew it was going to be an exciting day!

"Let's go," said Christie, leading Barbie out the door to the bright sunlight of the street. "We've got a long ride ahead of us."

Together they boarded a crowded bus and

headed into the desert. Along the way, more and more passengers got off the bus. After a while, Barbie and Christie were the only ones left. Finally the bus came to a stop at the edge of the desert.

"This is our stop!" Christie said as they stepped off the bus. Barbie and Christie stood at the edge of the road. They watched as the bus turned around and headed back toward the city.

"So where's the dig site?" Barbie asked. She looked out at the desert before her.

"We're not there yet," Christie replied. Then she walked over to a man dressed in layers of colorful cloth. Christie spoke a few words to him in **Arabic**. Then he disappeared behind a shack. A moment later, he returned leading three sleepy camels.

Barbie was speechless as Christie handed her the reins. "Climb aboard," Christie said.

"Camels?" Barbie laughed. "Wouldn't it be

faster to take a nice, air-conditioned car?"

"Don't worry," said Christie. Then she laughed at the look on Barbie's face. "This is how most of our team gets to the site every day. You'll get the hang of it in no time."

The camel kneeled down. Barbie carefully climbed on top of the animal. "You're more fun than a car, anyway," she said softly as she patted the camel's neck. The camel turned to look at her and snorted. Then the guide and Christie climbed on their camels. In a cloud of dust, the guide led Barbie and Christie farther into the desert.

To Barbie's surprise, the camels moved through the sand easily. Soon Barbie could see the pyramids come into view.

"Welcome to the Valley of Kings!" Christie exclaimed.

Barbie stared at the huge pyramids before her. They almost blocked out the bright sun. She had to lean back just to see the tops of them! Up

ahead lay the **sphinx**, the massive stone lion with the head of a man. It looked very serious, standing guard as it had for thousands of years.

When they came to a stop, the camels kneeled down again. Christie slid off and then helped Barbie down. The guide got off his camel, too. He took the reins of two of the animals and tied them together.

"Christie! *Marhaba*!" cried a young man, coming to greet them.

"Hello to you, too!" Christie said. "Barbie, this is Ahmed. He is the leader of our team. Ahmed helped discover the tomb we're going to explore."

"Hi, nice to meet you," Barbie said, shaking his hand.

Ahmed welcomed Barbie with a smile. "I'm so glad to meet you! Christie speaks of you often." Then he turned to Christie and said, "Is your friend going to be our canary?"

"What do you mean?" Barbie asked.

Christie grinned. "In 1923, an archaeologist named Howard Carter brought a pet canary with him on his search for King Tut's hidden tomb. The local Egyptians who helped him had never seen a golden bird with such a beautiful voice. They believed the bird had magical powers. People were sure it would bring them good luck in their search for the tomb. The search did not last long. Carter found the tomb right where they had camped!"

"And now we hope that your being here will bring us luck in finding the mysterious Treasure Room," Ahmed finished.

"Well, I don't know if I'll bring you any luck," Barbie replied. "But I'm glad to do anything I can to help you."

Ahmed politely held out his hand to her. "You are our guest," he said. "All you have to do is enjoy yourself. Now come along. We have

15

time for a quick tour of what we've found so far."
Taking his hand, Barbie stepped into the tomb.

Chapter Three

Barbie blinked, her eyes trying to get used to the darkness. Dim lightbulbs shone through a corridor, but she turned on her flashlight for a better look. She quickly realized that the stone walls were covered with pictures.

"Hieroglyphics," said Barbie. She ran her fingers across the wall, trying to imagine what story was told there.

"Look, this is the pharaoh," Christie said. "And here are his wife and children. He even had pet birds and dogs, from what I can see."

"And cats!" Barbie laughed, pointing to a

picture of a cat.

"This is the story of the pharaoh's life," Ahmed said. "He made sure no one would forget him, and it worked!"

Barbie studied the pictures, trying to understand them all. At last she stood up and smiled.

"The pharaoh was very grand," Barbie said. "But the workers who built this room must have been amazing, too. Just look at it!"

Ahmed nodded. "They were very talented," he agreed. "The builders planned the tomb to have hidden passages and tunnels. They wanted to trick robbers and keep them from taking the treasure. That's why it's so hard to find now!"

Just then a puff of dust and loose pebbles fell from the ceiling. Barbie and Christie jumped in surprise.

"Don't worry, it's safe in here," Ahmed said. "Things will move a bit, but there's nothing

to worry about. The Egyptians were expert builders. Besides, our people have also checked out everything. I've noticed a few mice in here, so the air is fresh and safe."

Then Ahmed took them to see what had been found on the other side of the tomb. Barbie followed Christie and Ahmed. Suddenly Barbie heard a muffled cry.

"What was that?" she wondered, quickly turning her head. Barbie walked toward the sound and listened carefully. She heard nothing. Shrugging, she turned to ask Ahmed and Christie if they heard the noise, too. But they were gone!

"Christie? Ahmed?" she called softly. The only reply was the strange crying sound again.

"I was right behind them!" Barbie thought, confused. "Where could they have gone?" But no one was there to answer her.

Barbie stumbled through a small doorway

into another room. "I had better stay put," she decided. "Once Christie and Ahmed realize I'm lost, they'll come back to get me. I just wish I knew what that crying sound was!"

Barbie shone her flashlight around. She couldn't believe her eyes. The room was filled with gleaming bowls of gold. Woven baskets held dried flowers and fruit. There were all kinds of carvings and statues. There were even pieces of furniture. But the walls were the most interesting thing about the room. The scenes on the walls were bright and alive. They seemed as if they had been painted only yesterday.

Then Barbie heard the noise again. This time it was louder and clearer. Her heart beat quickly. She pointed her flashlight toward the door, afraid of what she might see.

A little kitten ran into the room. "Why, hello there!" Barbie said in relief. The striped kitten rubbed against Barbie's legs, purring happily.

Barbie was grateful to meet such a cheerful little friend. The kitten would be company for her while she waited for Christie and Ahmed to return. "I wonder how you got in here," she said to the kitten. She picked it up and petted it gently. "You must have been so scared. Don't worry, I'll take care of you now." As if to say "thank you," the little cat licked her with its sandpapery tongue.

Barbie held the kitten, listening for sounds in the corridor. The minutes ticked past silently. Barbie started to wonder where Ahmed and Christie were. "I hope they're not lost, too," she said aloud.

Finally Barbie decided to stretch out on a long bench in the middle of the room. "I guess there's nothing we can do but wait," she said to the kitten, "so we might as well be comfortable." The cat yawned and curled up in a ball beside her. "Let's be patient," Barbie said. "I'm sure Ahmed and Christie will find us both soon." Suddenly

Barbie felt very tired. She closed her eyes and fell fast asleep next to her new friend.

Chapter Four

"Are you awake, Princess Barbie?" called a voice from the room next door.

Barbie opened her eyes and looked around. Sunlight poured through the window. It sparkled on the golden dishes laid out on a table before her. Beautiful paintings covered the walls. Birds and flowers brightened every corner.

Princess Christie walked barefoot into the room. She wore a long **linen** dress tied at the waist with a wide belt of woven gold. She had heavy bracelets on her wrists. On her head, she wore a gold crown.

"Good morning," said Barbie, hopping out of bed. She splashed cool water from a jug onto her face. Then she changed from her nightgown into a dress like the one Christie wore.

Together the princesses ate their breakfast. They had figs and poppy-seed cakes with sweet tea to drink. Outside, they could hear the singing voices of men in boats paddling up the Nile River. The men were going to work in the desert.

Barbie crossed the room to watch the boats go past. Because Barbie was a princess, none of the men dared to look up at her. Their minds could not stray from their job of building the pharaoh's pyramid and the sphinx. Princess Barbie knew this, but she wished that she could ask them about the work they did.

The pharaoh loved nothing more than talking about the building of his beloved pyramid. Each night, Barbie and Christie waited for the pharaoh to return home from overseeing the construction.

Secretly, they longed to see the pyramid up close. Barbie and Christie often asked the pharaoh to take them there. But he always refused.

Servants entered the room and cleared away the morning's dishes. Barbie and Christie smiled gratefully at them. The servants did not look at Barbie and Christie because of their high positions as princesses. Sometimes Barbie felt it was lonely to be royalty.

Barbie and Christie walked out into the palace courtyard. They wandered down to a shallow pool surrounded by tall **papyrus** plants. They took off their dresses. Underneath, they wore light cotton gowns. Christie eased into the cool, still water. Then Barbie got in and dunked under the surface. She swam over to Christie and surprised her.

"Oh!" cried Christie. "For a moment I thought you were a crocodile!"

Soon they were laughing and splashing

each other.

"Look!" Barbie exclaimed, suddenly standing. She pointed past the plants, toward the Nile just a few yards away.

Another boat was going past, and it carried a huge block of stone.

"I heard the sphinx is almost complete," Barbie said as the boat passed, "except for the face."

"Well," Christie sighed, "this may be the closest we'll ever get to it."

Barbie shaded her eyes and watched the boat grow smaller in the distance. "I hear that there are even drawings of us at the pyramids!"

"I know," Christie said. "I've heard there is one of us strumming our **lutes**, and another one of us weaving papyrus stems."

"Lutes!" Barbie cried. "We'd better practice! Once that sphinx's head is finished, there's going to be a big celebration. And we're expected to help entertain everyone!"

They got out of the pool and wrapped huge linen sheets around themselves. Then they returned to their rooms. After changing back into their dresses, they began to practice songs on their lutes. But as much as the princesses loved to sing, they were restless. Their eyes kept straying again and again to the Nile outside.

"Let's go there," Barbie said suddenly. "The two of us."

Christie looked at her. "Go where? To the pyramid? We're not allowed."

"I know," said Barbie. "But I would love to see the sphinx up close."

"You have the courage of a lion," Christie told her. "You know it is against palace rules to go. What if we are caught?"

"We won't get caught," Barbie told her as she plucked her lute. "Just leave everything to me." Suddenly a wrong note echoed throughout the room.

Christie giggled and said, "Maybe we should just stay here and practice a little."

Barbie agreed. "You're right," she said. "After that, I'll start the tapestry I'm making for the pharaoh. Perhaps there will be a place for it in the pyramid."

"I'm sure there will be," Christie replied. "Your weaving is always so beautiful."

The princesses practiced some more. Soon there was not a sour note to be heard. Next Barbie began to weave her tapestry. But her mind was racing. She was trying to come up with a plan for how they could see the sphinx tomorrow. There must be a way for her and Christie to go there without anyone finding out. After a while, Barbie smiled. She knew exactly what they would do!

Barbie wished the sun would set a little faster. She could hardly wait for their adventure to begin!

That night as she went to bed, Barbie looked toward the sky. "*Ra*," she whispered to the

Egyptian sun god who ruled day and night, "please come back early tomorrow!"

Chapter Five

The next morning, Princess Christie awoke when Princess Barbie began shaking her shoulder. The room was still dark and cool, and Christie wanted to go back to sleep.

"What's wrong?" Christie mumbled.

"Wake up!" Barbie said. "We're going to go see the pyramids for ourselves today."

"Are you really serious about this?" Christie replied. "We will get into terrible trouble with the pharaoh."

"He'll never know," answered Barbie. "Now put this on! Quickly!"

Christie sleepily rubbed her eyes and sat up. She reached for the rough robe Barbie held out to her. The heavy fabric was itchy and smelly.

"I found these clothes at the stable," Barbie explained. She tied a cord around her waist. "Now we'll look just like the pharaoh's workers!"

Christie gazed at the shiny bracelets and linen dress she would normally wear. But she knew there would be no changing Barbie's mind. She slipped into the robe and sandals and followed Barbie outside.

As members of the Egyptian royal family, Princess Barbie and Princess Christie had led special lives. They'd never even been outside the palace alone before. So their hearts pounded as they sneaked out of the palace gate. In the east, the sun was beginning to rise.

Barbie had told one of their servants about their plan. Just as the servant had promised, one of the pharaoh's camels was tied to a tree near the riverbank. The camel knelt down as Barbie and Christie climbed up onto its back. Then they headed in the direction of the construction.

As the camel walked along, the Nile quickly filled with boats of workers on their way to the pyramid and sphinx. In fields nearby, men and women tended crops in the morning sun.

"It is so hot already," Barbie said, wiping her forehead. "Let's stop for a minute and have a drink."

First Barbie guided the camel to the river so it could sip some water. Then she led it to the cool shade of a palm tree to rest.

Barbie and Christie walked to the river's edge and scooped up a bowl of water for themselves. Suddenly they heard a strange noise.

"What could that be?" Christie cried.

Barbie went to **investigate**. She walked over to the water and parted the papyrus reeds. She was careful to keep an eye out for crocodiles and snakes. She hoped the noise had been made by a river bird.

"Barbie? Do you see anything?" Christie called.

Barbie began to laugh. "Look what I found!" she cried. She came from behind the grasses. In her arms was a tiny wet kitten. Christie sighed in relief.

"It must be hungry," Christie said. "See how thin it is!"

"Poor thing!" Barbie cooed as she fed the kitten some of her lunch. "What you need is a good meal. I bet you need a good home to go with it! Don't worry, I will make sure you have someone to take care of you."

Barbie carefully tucked the kitten into the large hamper she was carrying. Then she strapped it to the camel's side.

"Well, this adventure is off to a good start," Barbie told Christie brightly. "What good fortune

it was for us to find a cat!"

Christie agreed. Everyone in Egypt believed cats brought good luck. With smiling faces, the two friends headed toward the sphinx again.

Getting closer, Barbie and Christie saw hundreds of workers carrying huge boulders from the boats to the work site. Hundreds more were carrying smaller rocks back and forth.

Nearby, **sculptors** carefully carved rocks into statues of all sizes. Soon Barbie and Christie had to pull their cloth scarves over their mouths. They never realized how much dust the stone carvers made!

"Come on," said Barbie. The camel knelt down and she and Christie got off. Barbie carefully lifted the cat out of the hamper. "Let's get a closer look."

No one seemed to notice the two young women making their way through the work site. Everyone was too busy.

"There it is!" Barbie cried. The friends ran in the sand toward the huge body of the great sphinx they had heard so much about. Barbie and Christie were speechless. Never in their lives had they seen anything so grand!

"No! No! No!" a voice suddenly shouted. Barbie and Christie turned around and gasped. There stood the pharaoh himself, just a few yards away! Barbie and Christie hurried behind a large slab of stone nearby.

"That was a close one!" Christie said.

"Too close!" agreed Barbie.

A frightened young man bowed before the pharaoh. Barbie noticed that the man held out a sheet of **parchment** with the head of an eagle sketched on it.

"My humblest apologies, Pharaoh," the man whispered. But the pharaoh just took the parchment and crumpled it in his fist.

The pharaoh shook his head in disgust. "Is

there no one in all of Egypt who can sketch the face of the sphinx?" he cried. Then he stormed away, grumbling to himself.

Even Barbie and Christie felt scared. They had never seen him so angry.

The young artist hung his head. "It is impossible," he said. "The pharaoh will never be pleased with *any* sketch."

Chapter Six

Seconds later, the cat jumped out of Barbie's arms. It ran up to a ragged young man standing on the edge of the work site. He looked different than the rest of the men who walked about. He held no hammer or **chisel** like the others. Instead he carried a roll of paper under his arm.

"I wonder who that is," Barbie whispered to Christie.

As they watched, the young man began to sketch. Barbie and Christie quietly made their way over to him.

"May we see what you are drawing?"

Barbie asked.

Shyly, the man showed her his sketch.

"Why, it's the cat!" Christie exclaimed.

"Is this cat yours?" asked the man.

"No," replied Barbie. "In fact, he needs a home," she hinted.

"Well, why not?" said the man, laughing. "Maybe he'll bring me good luck."

Just then Christie saw the pharaoh heading back their way. "Oh, no! Not again!" she cried. "We'd better hide!"

Quickly Barbie and Christie raced behind the slab of stone again and hid.

"You there! Let me see that!" demanded the pharaoh, taking the paper.

The pharaoh looked at the sketch. He liked the detail and how alive the cat in the drawing seemed.

"You are more talented than any of the royal artists here. Quickly now! Show me what else you can do! Draw the face for my great sphinx by the time I return!" ordered the pharaoh. Then he walked away.

After the pharaoh had gone, Barbie and Christie once again walked over to the artist. "What shall I do?" he moaned. "No one has been able to please him! Why should he like my sketch?"

Barbie shook her head. "I think I know what will work," she said. Then she shared her idea of the perfect sketch for the face of the sphinx. A big grin appeared on the young man's face, and he started to draw.

"I hate to spoil the fun," said Christie, "but we can't take another chance that the pharaoh might see us. I think we'd better go home."

"You're right," said Barbie. "At least we finally saw the pyramids and the sphinx!"

So Barbie and Christie said good-bye to the young man and headed back to the palace.

Not long after the princesses had gone, the

pharaoh came back. "Let me see what you have done!" he demanded.

The young man bowed before him. He gave the pharaoh his sketch.

Workers and other artists gathered around. Normally, no one was allowed to approach the pharaoh unless they were called for. But everyone was so curious, they forgot about the rules.

Suddenly the pharaoh lifted the design above his head for all to see. "At last!" he cried. There was a perfect drawing of the pharaoh's own face!

"At last! At last!" the pharaoh said over and over again. "I have a face for the sphinx!" Then he turned back to the artist. "As a reward for your drawing, you shall live at the palace and work as one of the royal artists!"

The young man was surprised and grateful. But when he opened his mouth to speak, a "meow!" was heard.

"Meow! Meow!" cried the kitten at their

feet. The tiny cat blinked in the bright sunshine.

The pharaoh threw back his head and laughed. All the workers dropped their tools and listened in shock. The pharaoh had never laughed in front of them before!

"Who is this?" asked the pharaoh. He pointed to the kitten.

The young man thought quickly. "A present for you, Pharaoh," he said, picking up the cat.

The pharaoh took the purring cat and stroked it. "This cat will hold a place of honor at the palace. And to mark this day, I shall have a statue of it made to be placed in the pyramid."

Chapter Seven

Back at the palace, Princesses Barbie and Christie changed out of their **disguises**. They couldn't wait until the pharaoh returned home that evening. They wanted to know what had happened with the young artist and his drawing.

Christie smiled. "I'll bet the pharaoh has some important news to share with us tonight!" she said.

Barbie agreed as she slipped her robe over her head. She was happy to be out of the dusty clothes.

Suddenly loud voices filled the halls as the

pharaoh stepped from his royal boat. Musicians began to play. Plates and goblets were brought out as the table in the main room was set for a banquet.

"Let's go and greet him," Christie said.

Barbie and Christie joined the others gathered before the pharaoh. They slowly made their way to the front. They didn't want to miss a single detail as the pharaoh told of the day's events.

After the pharaoh had shown the drawing, he asked Princess Barbie to come closer. A servant produced a basket. The pharaoh took out the kitten. As he handed it to Princess Barbie he said, "Perhaps it was this little creature who brought good luck to my artist today. Take good care of him!"

Once again, Barbie held the tiny kitten in her arms. She was surprised but pleased to have her little friend with her again. She bowed to the pharaoh. Then the music began, and the pharaoh left for the banquet hall.

"I'd better bring you someplace quiet," Barbie said to the kitten. "You've had enough excitement for one day!"

Barbie and Christie went back to Barbie's bedchamber. A soft breeze drifted through the open window. The sun was setting, and the sky glowed red and gold.

The kitten sat beside Barbie as Christie prepared to go back to the party.

"I'll catch up with you in a few minutes," Barbie said wearily. "It's been such a busy day, and I'm very tired. I just want to rest for a moment."

"All right. I'll see you in a little while," Christie called as she left the room.

But Barbie didn't hear her. She and the kitten were already fast asleep.

Chapter Eight

Noises from the corridor seemed to be drawing closer. Barbie thought she heard her name being called. She didn't know how long she had slept, but the gentle touch of the kitten rubbing against her arm made her sit straight up.

"Oh, my!" she said, rubbing her eyes. "What a dream that was!"

The kitten purred, its eyes glowing in the darkness. They were in the tomb. Christie and Ahmed were still not there.

Barbie felt around for her flashlight. As the light shone, the treasures of the room glowed, despite their layers of dust. The kitten jumped to the floor and ran to the doorway.

"Barbie?" a voice said in the darkness.

"Here I am!" Barbie called, flashing the light beam beyond the doorway. "Follow the narrow passageway!"

The kitten chased after the moving light beam, trying to catch it with its paws. In a moment the cat was back, this time followed by Christie and Ahmed!

"Thank goodness!" Christie cried, giving Barbie a hug. "We were so worried about you!"

"I'm so glad you found me!" exclaimed Barbie. "I should have stayed right next to you. How long have I been in here? It felt like thousands of years!"

"We've been searching for an hour," Ahmed said, his eyes looking around the room.

"Oh, dear," Barbie said. "I hope I didn't delay your expedition."

But Ahmed was not listening. He was wandering around the room as if he were sleepwalking.

"Christie, look!" he called. He shone his flashlight all around the room.

Now Christie had joined Ahmed. Together they looked at the golden statues, the carvings, the coins, and the furniture.

Barbie watched her friends explore all the treasures in the room. A strange feeling came over her. These objects seemed as normal to her as her camera.

"Ahmed, do you know whose face is on the sphinx?" Barbie asked him suddenly.

Ahmed smiled. "Of course," he replied. "It is the face of a great pharaoh."

Barbie nodded. "I thought so," she said.

Christie opened a large chest full of jewelry. "Ahmed, are you thinking what I'm thinking?" she said.

Ahmed nodded excitedly. "Yes, Christie," he said. "There can be no other explanation. This must be—"

"The Treasure Room!" they all shouted.

"It might have taken us months to find it on our own!" Ahmed said to Barbie. "Just like Howard Carter's canary, you *did* bring us luck!"

"If I didn't know any better, I'd say you had secret knowledge of the ancient Egyptians!" Christie exclaimed.

Barbie ran her hand across the hieroglyphic of Egyptian princesses. "Hmm! Maybe I do!" she said softly.